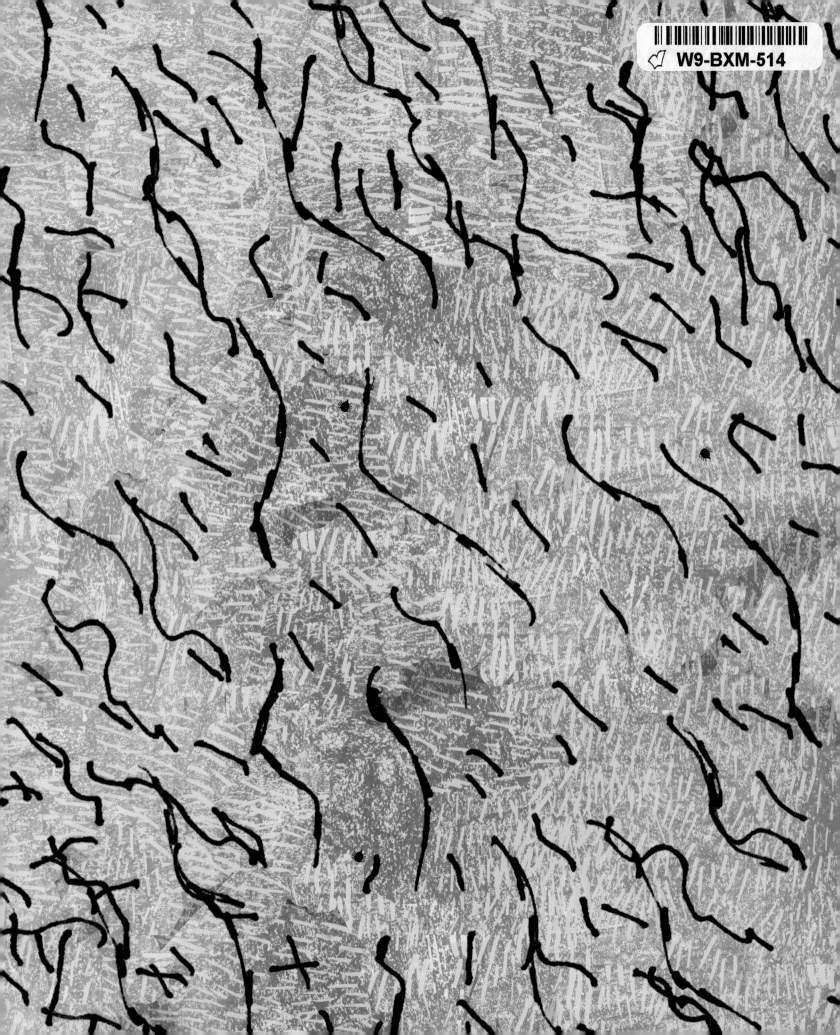

For Karen – ST
For Penny – HS

This isn't a new story. It is my retelling of a folktale which
has been around for more than 2000 years. Versions of the story
have been recorded in countries as far apart as Ireland, South Africa,
Iran, China and the USA. And I'd like to start by raising my hat
to the storytellers who passed it on to us now. S.T.

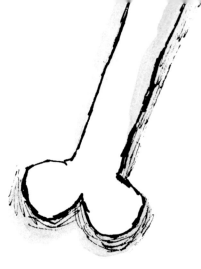

JANETTA OTTER-BARRY BOOKS

The Grizzly Bear with the Frizzly Hair copyright © Frances Lincoln Limited 2011
Text copyright © Sean Taylor 2011
Illustrations copyright © Hannah Shaw 2011
The right of Sean Taylor and Hannah Shaw to be identified respectively as the author
and illustrator of this work has been asserted by them in accordance with
the Copyright, Designs and Patents Act, 1988 (United Kingdom).

First published in Great Britain and in the USA in 2011 by
Frances Lincoln Children's Books, 4 Torriano Mews,
Torriano Avenue, London NW5 2RZ
www.franceslincoln.com

A catalogue record for this book is available from the British Library.
ISBN 978-1-84780-085-5

Illustrated with pen and ink and scanned textures
Typeset in Dominican and Rough Typewriter

Printed in Dongguan, Guangdong, China by South China Printing in December 2010

1 3 5 7 9 8 6 4 2

The Grizzly Bear with the Frizzly Hair

Retold by
Sean Taylor

Illustrated by
Hannah Shaw

F

FRANCES LINCOLN
CHILDREN'S BOOKS

BEWARE OF THE BEAR

There was nothing left to eat in the woods.
The Grizzly Bear with the Frizzly Hair had eaten it all.

That's why he was
bad-tempered and hungry.
That's why he was on the prowl.

The Grizzly Bear
with the Frizzly Hair

could frighten the feathers off a peacock.

He could startle the
whiskers off a walrus.

He could
scare the
stripes off
a tiger.

So how do you think this itzy-bitzy rabbit felt, when they came

FACE to FACE?

"Yipes!" blinked the rabbit.
"What are you going to do?"

"Have my lunch," growled the bear.
"And my lunch is...

YOU!"

Then he opened his frizzly, grizzly mouth
and dangled the rabbit inside.

"You're going to eat my toes!"
said the rabbit.

"Please do not! Those toes there...
are the favourite ones I've got!"

"Tough!"
growled the bear.

"That's how it goes!
I'm hungry and those
look like...

VERY TASTY
TOES!"

He opened his frizzly, grizzly mouth a little wider.

"Not my knees!"
said the rabbit.

"Please!
For heaven's sake!
They're ever so very bony
And you'll get a tummy ache!"

"Not my tum-tum-tummy!" said the rabbit,

"or my ch-ch-chest!
If you eat up those,
there'll be hardly
anything left!"

He opened his frizzly, grizzly mouth a little wider.

"My head!" squeaked the rabbit.
"Wait! Not yet! Don't bite!
Eating someone's head is
really not... polite!"

"I'm not
POLITE!"
roared the bear.

"I'm RUDE!
Everyone knows!

And I hope you've enjoyed
the story because
THIS IS AS FAR
AS IT GOES!"

The frizzly, grizzly mouth
started to close.
Our itzy-bitzy friend quivered
down to his marrow bone jelly.

In fact, he could have just shut his eyes...
and shrivelled with fright... and given up.

But he didn't.

"Look behind you!" he yelled.
"An elephant's coming! LOOK!"

"Quiet!" growled the bear.

"That's the oldest trick in the book!"

"I know a joke!" tried the rabbit. "It's going to make you laugh!"

"NO!" bristled the bear.

"I'M GOING TO BITE YOU IN HALF."

MORE BEAR JOKES

Q: Why do bears have fur coats?

A: Because they'd look very silly in anoraks

HA!
HA!

"But I'm tiny," the rabbit babbled.
"I'll be gone in one munch!

FRIZZLY GRIZZLY CAVE

ENTER AT YOUR OWN RISK

Wouldn't you maybe...
rather... have
a really BIG lunch?"

FAIRY STORIES FOR LITTLE BEARS

Giant Bear Lunches

MUCH BIGGER SNACKS

"END OF STORY!"
snarled the bear.

"I don't want your maybes!
What do you think this is...

A BEDTIME BOOK FOR BABIES?"

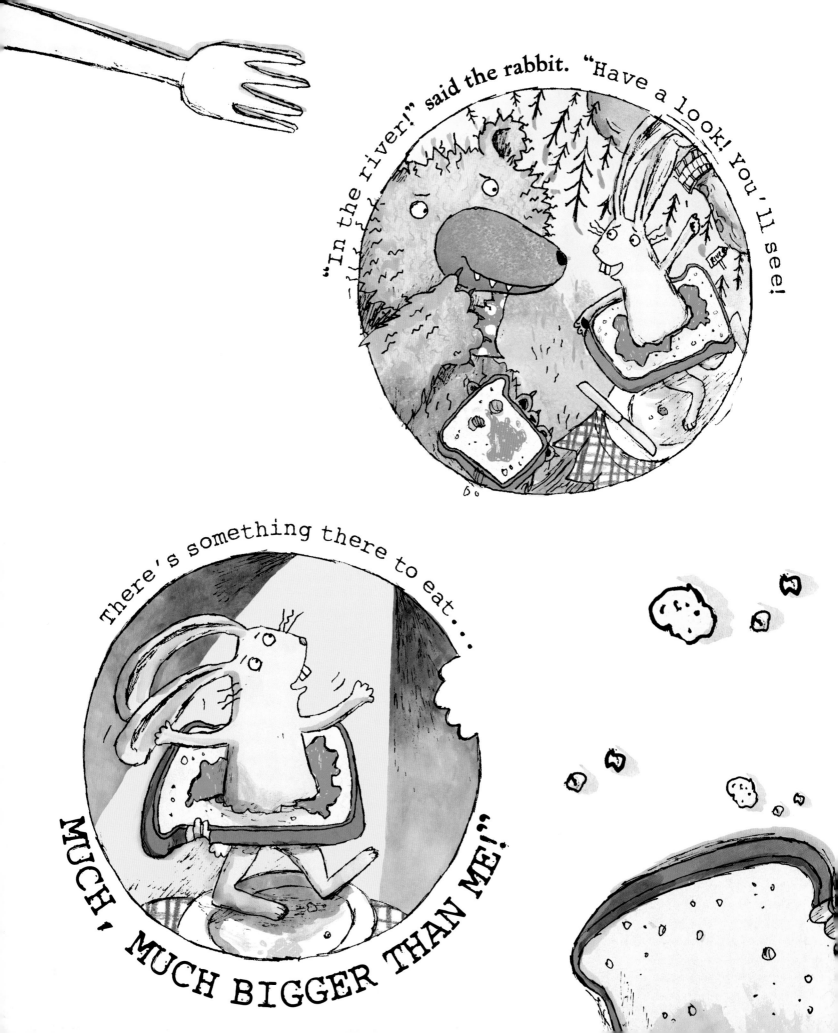

'Much, much bigger?"
muttered the bear.

"Hmmmmmm…"

He kept a tight hold on the rabbit
but he walked back through the woods
and… took a little look in the river.

What was that?
It was the strangest...frizzliest...
grizzliest thing he'd ever seen.
But it did look very filling
compared to a rabbit.

"Delicious!"
blinked the rabbit.
"Succulent, scrumptious and yummy!
Imagine how good you'd feel
with all of that in your tummy!"

The Grizzly Bear with the Frizzly Hair
dropped the rabbit and
he grabbed at the thing in the river.
But it grabbed straight back.

He bared his teeth.
But it bared its teeth back.

"Oh dear!" sighed the rabbit.
"I'll tell you what I think.
It reckons you are
just some...
GREAT BIG
GOOFY WIMP!"

The Grizzly Bear with Frizzly Hair
swiped a giant paw at the thing
in the river.

But the thing in the river
swiped a giant paw back.

That was too much.

In a rage, the bear jumped
at his own reflection.

And he sank deep down into the water.

Deep...

down...

into...

the water.

The rabbit didn't hang about. He went skittling off as fast as he could.

"COME BACK!" gurgled the bear, wrinkling his soggy nose.

"I hope you enjoyed the story," called the rabbit, "BECAUSE THIS IS AS FAR AS IT GOES!"

RABBIT LAND welcome

And with that he was gone, safely into the long grass,

checking his toes,
checking his knees,
checking his tummy, his chest and his head.

And they were
all still there!

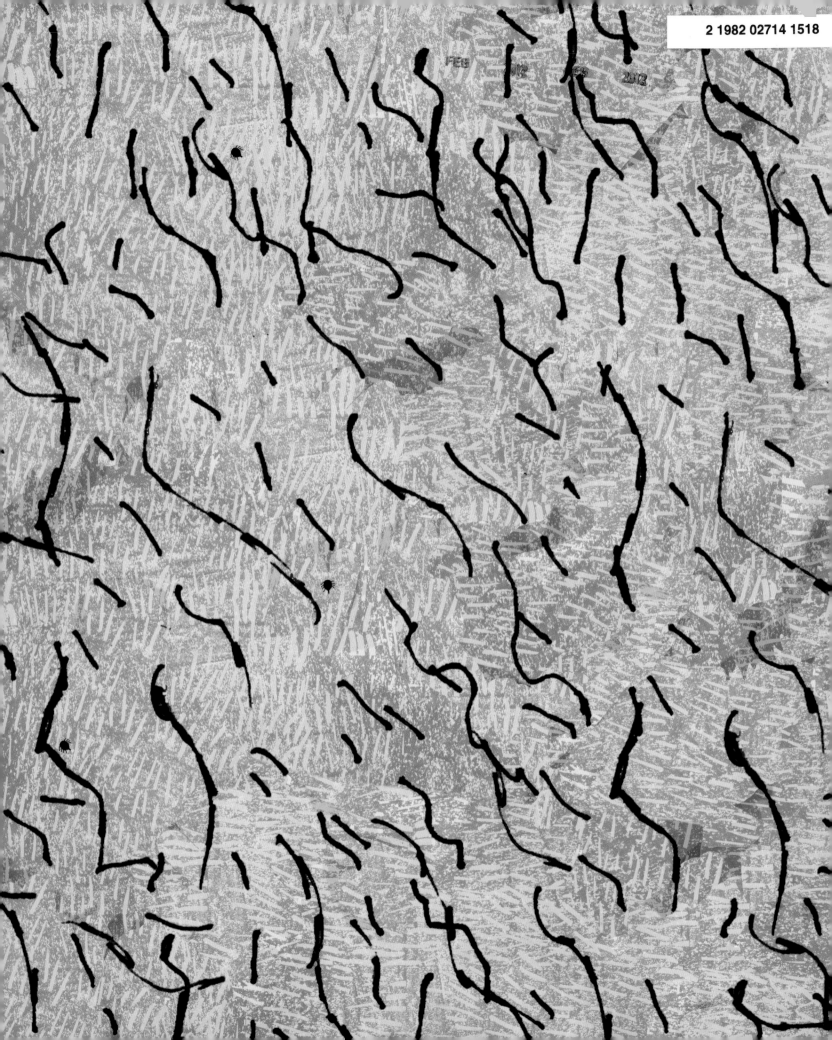